THE MYSTERY
OF THE
Graveyard
of the
Atlantic

Managing Editor: Sherry Moss
Senior Editor: Janice Baker
Assistant Editor: Michael Kelly
Cover Design: Vicki DeJoy
Cover Photo Credits: ©Dirk-Jan Matlaar, istockphoto, ©Jupiterimages Corporation
Picture Credits: Vicki DeJoy
Content Design and Illustrations: Randolyn Friedlander

Gallopade International is introducing SAT words that kids need to know in
each new book that we publish. The SAT words are bold in the story. Look
for this special logo beside each word in the glossary. Happy Learning!

Gallopade is proud to be a member and supporter of these educational organizations
and associations:

American Booksellers Association
American Library Association
International Reading Association
National Association for Gifted Children
The National School Supply and Equipment Association
The National Council for the Social Studies
Museum Store Association
Association of Partners for Public Lands
Association of Booksellers for Children
Association for the Study of African American Life and History
National Alliance of Black School Educators

Once upon a time…

Hmm, kids keep asking me to write a mystery book. What shall I do?

Mimi

Write one about spiders!

5

You two really are characters, that's all I've got to say!

Yes you are! And, of course I choose you! But what should I write about?

 National Parks!

 SCARY PLACES!

FAMOUS PLACES!

FUN PLACES!

Disney World!

New York City!

Dracula's Castle

GRAND CANYON

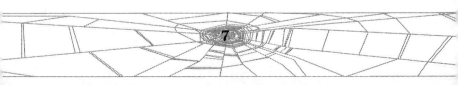

On the *Mystery Girl* airplane ...

I can FLY US anywhere!

Or aboard
the *Mimi!*

Take me to the
Forbidden City!

Or by surfboard,
rickshaw,
motorbike,
camel ...

All great ideas!
I can put a lot of history,

MYSTERY,

legend, lore, and **laughs** in
the books! We can use other boys and girls
in the books. It will be educational and fun!

Good
stuff!

9

And so, Mimi, Papa, Christina, and Grant took off aboard the *Mystery Girl* and America's National Mystery Book Series—where the adventure is real and so are the characters! —was born.

START YOUR ADVENTURE TODAY!

ABOUT THE CHARACTERS

Christina
Yother
Age 10

Grant
Yother
Age 7

Kyle
O'Connor
Age 12

Leah
Clark
Age 7

1
TAKEOFF

"Some of my fondest childhood memories are of the fun I had at Cape Hatteras," Mimi said, twisting around in the front seat of the plane to look at her granddaughter, Christina. "The ocean, beaches, sandbars, and history of the Outer Banks fascinated me."

"Is that why you want to write a mystery about Cape Hatteras?" Christina asked, leaning forward from her back seat.

"Yes!" Mimi said. "But I want you and your brother to experience all the things I did. My friends and I would take a rowboat out to the sandbars and search for seashells. Sometimes we'd row to another island reef to search for treasure."

"Sounds kind of boring," Christina said.

"Not at all," Mimi said, winking. "We'd always find something that entertained us. We found an island of wild ponies, and snorkeled through several incredible shipwrecks at Diamond Shoals, just off Cape Hatteras."

"How old were you?" Christina asked.

"About your age," Mimi said. "Maybe just a couple of years older."

"So," Christina said, smiling, "can Grant and I go row boating by ourselves?"

Mimi shook her head. "I don't think so!" she said. "You're not familiar with the area and with boats. I think you'll need to wait until you're a little bit older."

CLANK!

Christina looked out the front windshield. Papa had closed the right side engine cowl. "I thought you'd say that," she said.

Papa opened the left engine cowl on the *Mystery Girl*, his little red and white airplane that he used to fly his wife, Mimi, a children's mystery book writer, and him wherever they wanted to travel. There were times, like today, when their two grandchildren, Christina and Grant, joined them on a trip.

After performing his pre-flight check of the engine compartment, Papa closed the cowl and tightened the locking thumbscrews.

"Everything okay?" Grant asked, as he scurried up to Papa's side.

"Yep!" Papa said. "Where are Christina and your grandmother?"

Grant pointed toward the plane's cockpit.

Papa looked up and saw them seated inside the plane, talking. "Huh!" he huffed. "I didn't notice them get on board. I wonder where they put their bags?"

Even though his mind was elsewhere, Grant pointed to the back of the plane. Mimi's red suitcase and Christina's pink bag sat on the ground by the door to the small cargo compartment.

Papa spied the luggage and nodded. "What's wrong?" he asked. "Cat got your tongue today?"

"No, sir!" Grant said, smiling. "I don't let anything around my tongue except food. I was thinking about the Outer Banks and remembered something I learned in school."

As Papa unlatched the cargo door, Grant lifted one of the suitcases. He handed the bag to his grandfather. "I seem to remember something about a ship made of iron sinking along the Outer Banks," Grant recalled.

"Well," Papa remarked, "you must be talking about the USS *Monitor*, which was an ironclad ship developed by the North during the Civil War. It went down just off Cape Hatteras, which is where we're going to be staying."

"What does 'iron glad' mean?" Grant asked. "Was the ship glad about something?"

"It's iron*clad*, Grant," Papa corrected, smiling. "It was the first ship built with an all-iron hull, which protected it from the cannon fire that sank ordinary wooden ships. It kind of looked like an armored raft with most of the hull under water."

"How did it happen?" Grant asked.

"How did what happen?" Papa replied, trying to cram one of Mimi's overstuffed suitcases through the small cargo door opening. "She's probably stuffed this thing full of shoes again," he muttered.

"How did the ironclad ship go down?" Grant asked again.

Papa latched the door and leaned up against it. He adjusted the cowboy hat he always wore, along with his chocolate-brown boots and jeans. "Well, first of all," he explained, "the *Monitor* was not only the first all-iron ship built by the North, but the first ship to have a rotating gun turret. But that gun was of no help on the night it sunk. I believe it was around Christmas in 1862.

"The *Monitor* was rounding Cape Hatteras during a vicious storm at a spot the locals call the Graveyard of the Atlantic," Papa continued. "It was right near Diamond Shoals, which is 'ground zero' for shipwrecks."

"Diamond shores?" Grant asked. "Are there diamonds there?"

"Not shores," Papa said. "Shoals! It's an enormous area of sneaky, shifting sandbars that snatch ships, causing them to run aground and sink! The *Monitor* got trapped in those fingers, and only a handful of the crew survived."

"It must be a scary place," Grant observed, with a worried frown spreading across his face.

"It can be," Papa said. "They say that during an Outer Banks storm, you can stand on shore and watch two oceans clash because the northbound Gulf Stream runs right smack into the cold currents coming down from the Arctic."

Grant's blue eyes were wide with anticipation. "What happens then, Papa?" he asked.

"When they collide," Papa said, "an explosion of water spews up to 100 feet into the sky, taking sand, shells, and sea life with it, and then dumping them back into the sea, just so it can repeat it over and over again."

"Coooooool," Grant sighed.

"Up and down the Outer Banks," Papa continued, "the skeletons of at least 500 ships lie buried. Some are covered only by water, with a single piece of metal protruding above the surface to mark their final resting places. Others have been covered in sand from the storm that sunk them."

"Wow!" Grant said. "Do you think some of the ships had gold onboard?"

"A lot of those sunken ships carried goods like coffee and sugar, or salt and spices," Papa said. "But there were many ships, like the Spanish treasure ships returning to Spain from the mines of Mexico and South America, that carried gold, silver, and jewels."

Papa tousled Grant's blonde curls. "Even today," he said, "divers and treasure hunters still look for sunken treasure there."

"Awesome!" Grant exclaimed, as he climbed into the plane. "I love shipwrecks. I think I'll be one of those treasure hunters when I grow up!"

CLICK!

With his seatbelt fastened, Grant had a sudden image of himself standing on the bridge of a treasure hunting ship. A large chest, filled with overflowing gold coins, sat at his feet.

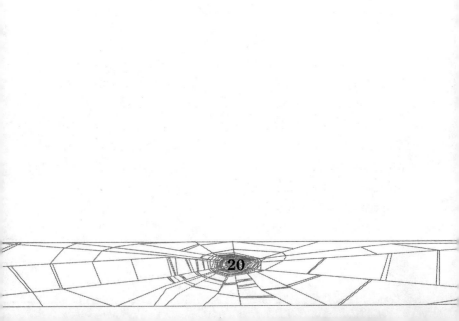

20

2
THUNDER, CLATTER, BOOM, BOOM, BOOM

Grant squirmed in his seat. Christina slept curled up in a ball next to him, her long brown hair spilling over her face. He grabbed the headset from the hook next to his seat and placed it over his ears. He pulled the microphone close to his mouth and pressed the transmit key. "Papa, are we there yet?" he whined.

The last rays of sun had disappeared over the western horizon about twenty minutes earlier. "Hang in there, big guy," Papa replied, gazing out the front windshield. "We're about 20 miles out."

The *Mystery Girl* had already descended beneath a blanket of clouds, which magically appeared a few minutes earlier, and was on final approach to the airport. Papa scanned the sky in front of him for runway lights, but still couldn't see any.

PING! PING!

Hard rain began to pelt the airplane, slowly at first, and then became a thunderous roar.

The noise awoke Christina. She uncurled and stretched. "What's going on?" she asked. "Is that rain? It's really coming down hard!"

"Yes, dear!" Mimi said. "Just relax! Papa's got it under control."

RAT! TAT! TAT!

THUMP!
BANG!

Mimi and Christina screamed, as Grant pushed the headset's earpieces against his head to block out their ear-piercing shrieks.

"HANG ON!" Papa bellowed, pushing the yoke forward, and nosing the airplane down slightly.

"What was that?" Mimi shouted, looking back at Christina and Grant. "Are you two okay?"

Christina and Grant nodded their heads silently, their eyes wide with apprehension.

"Birds!" Papa yelled, his knuckles turning white as he struggled to hold the yoke steady. Scanning his instruments, he said, "We flew through a flock of birds." The plane pitched up and down and slid left and right as turbulence shook it violently around the sky.

Christina leaned over and tightened Grant's seatbelt. They looked at each other and clasped hands.

The turbulence grew worse with each passing second. "We've got to land!" Mimi shouted.

Papa couldn't see the runway lights at all. They were still 10 miles from the airport. The *Mystery Girl* began to sputter. He looked down at his fuel gage and saw the digital readout dropping rapidly.

"That's not good!" Papa said. "It looks like a bird broke through the air screen and took out the fuel line."

"Kids, put on your life jackets—NOW!" Papa shouted, as the aircraft skimmed just 200 feet above the violent waves beneath them.

FLASH! BOOM!

Lightning lit the sky and powerful vibrations thundered, like an immense bowling ball smashing into electrically charged bowling pins.

Christina helped Grant fasten the buckle on his bright yellow life jacket. She grabbed his hand again. "It'll be all right!" she said to her wide-eyed little brother.

Grant shook his head up and down. "I know!" he said. "Papa won't let anything bad happen."

"Come on, girl," Papa shouted to the *Mystery Girl*. "Just a little bit further." Now they were just five miles from the airport.

Suddenly, the engine stopped! The immediate silence was frightening.

"I'm going to try and land on the beach," Papa said. "Hold on tight, because I can't see a thing."

"What's that?" Mimi shouted, as two foggy lights appeared in front of them.

"Well, I'll be!" Papa said. "Someone's on the beach, showing us where to land!"

As the *Mystery Girl* floated quietly down toward the lights, without any power, the rain began to lighten and the fog began to lift. Papa watched the lights gently bounce up and down. He realized that the person waving the lights was not on the beach, but in a small boat. Now he could see the beach 50 yards off to his left, but didn't have enough altitude to turn the plane toward it.

As the *Mystery Girl* flew over the lights, Papa shouted, "Brace yourselves, we're going in!"

"Look!" Mimi shouted, pointing out the front windshield. "There's a sandbar!"

"I see it!" Papa said, pulling back lightly on the yoke to keep them in the air just a few seconds longer. The *Mystery Girl* glided down onto the sandbar just 20 feet from the water. She sped silently through the hard packed sand and came to a stop.

Papa and Mimi immediately turned to look at Christina and Grant. They were both wide-eyed and ghostly white.

Grant suddenly relaxed. "That was awesome!" he said, with a big grin.

Christina craned her neck to look out the window. *I wonder where that boat is, she thought. Who was out there, lighting our way? Goosebumps crept up her arms. She had a feeling something mysterious was waiting for them in Cape Hatteras!*

3
A FATEFUL FALL

"That was some great flying, Papa," Grant said. "I knew you'd get us down safe."

"You did great, Papa," Christina agreed. "But, let's not do that again!" She looked out the window once more. "What about the person in the little boat? They may need help!"

Papa looked at Mimi, who was patting her blond curls back into place after all the excitement. "Christina's right. The rain has stopped so I'll go check—"

"Not by yourself!" Mimi interrupted. "I'll go with you!"

"Hey," Christina added. "Grant and I don't want to stay here by ourselves! Can we go, too?"

"All right!" Papa replied. "But we all have to stay close together so we don't get separated in this fog. Do you understand?"

Christina and Grant nodded.

"Let's take off our shoes then," Papa suggested.

"Holy moley!" Grant said, as he crawled out of the plane into the thick, hot, muggy North Carolina evening. "This is like taking a steam bath!" He wiped away the sweat that instantly appeared on his forehead.

"Let's go this way," Papa said, heading back to where the plane had touched down.

Although the rain had stopped, the wind gusted strongly. Christina was having trouble keeping up. The turbulent roar of the ocean and the howling wind alarmed her. Each strong gust threatened to blow over her slender frame. Plus, she couldn't remember a time she had sweat so much. Who would want to live in a place like this, she thought.

Grant was also having second thoughts about leaving the airplane. Every few seconds he had to wipe sweat from his eyes. Between the sweat and the salty ocean air, his eyes began to burn. The fog blew around in patches, but every now and then, he caught a glimpse of the washing-machine ocean, churning the water around violently. He was thankful they'd made it to land safely. A warm gust of wind pushed him backwards, sending shivers up his spine.

"I think I see something!" Papa shouted, as he jogged down the packed sand.

Everyone ran after Papa, trying to keep up. Suddenly, he disappeared!

"WHOOOOAAA!"

"Papa!" Mimi called. "What happened?" She put her arms out to grab Grant and Christina's hands.

"Mimi!" Papa shouted. "Be careful, there's a drop-off!"

Mimi, Christina, and Grant appeared at the edge of the short embankment that Papa had fallen off and scurried down to him.

"Are you okay?" Grant asked, reaching his grandfather's side first.

"Ahh!" Papa said. "I think I twisted my ankle."

Mimi felt down Papa's leg until she reached his already swollen ankle.

"OWWWW!"

Papa screamed.

Mimi lightened her touch. "It's okay," she said, in a calm voice. "But you did more than sprain your ankle. It might be broken."

Something caught Christina's eye. *Was that a light twinkling just over the embankment? Or was it another lightning flash in the distance? This place was getting more mysterious by the minute!*

30

4
BIRDS OF A FEATHER

A loud wave crashed just behind Papa. "We need to get you back to the *Mystery Girl* so I can call for help," Mimi said.

"Yeah," Papa agreed, as salty mist hit him in the face. "If you can help me to my good foot, I think I can make it up the embankment."

A few minutes and several loud grunts later, Mimi, Christina, and Grant had helped Papa get to the hard packed sandbar. The group trudged slowly toward the airplane.

"Did anyone see the mystery man in the boat?" Papa asked, trying to take the focus off his unfortunate accident.

They all shook their heads. "I don't think it was a man in a boat," Grant announced.

Everyone looked at him.

"But there had to be someone in the boat," Christina said.

"I don't know," Grant said. "I think we saw something as we passed over the lights, but it wasn't a man."

Papa had his arm around Grant's shoulder. "If it wasn't a man, what was it?" he asked.

"I think we all saw a ghost!" Grant maintained. "Or maybe a guiding angel."

"Maybe you're right," Christina said, remembering her funny feeling.

"Humph," Papa said. "I didn't see any wings on that angel."

SCCRRRIIEEEKKK!

"What's that?" Grant shouted, tightening his grip on Papa's waist. The gusting wind grew louder.

"There's something out there!" Christina said.

Like a curtain, the swirling fog parted in front of them, revealing the *Mystery Girl*. A gust of wind slammed the airplane's rudder over to the side. The wind shrieked as it cut over the rudder's thin edge.

"Ha!" Papa said, chuckling. "It's just the rudder."

Wow! A talking parrot!

34

"No!" Grant exclaimed. "That's not it! Listen!"

SQUAWK! SQUAWK!

Suddenly, through the foggy mist, a multicolored Macaw parrot flew toward them. It was stunning to behold, with a scarlet head and body, and yellow wings tipped in royal blue. Squawking loudly, its wings flapped gracefully through the wind gusts. It landed on the *Mystery Girl's* wing.

SQUAWK!

Grant jumped when a high-pitched voice came from the bird.

The bird's eyes blinked, and it bobbed its head up and down. "Survive the shoals, and you'll see it clearly," it repeated.

SQUAWK! SQUAWK!

The parrot took flight and disappeared into the fog.

"What in the world..." Papa said, amazed.

Christina stared into the fog after the bird. "See what clearly?" she asked. "What's that supposed to mean?"

Papa propped himself against the plane. Mimi climbed into the cockpit, turned on the radio, and picked up the microphone to call the Coast Guard for help.

"I don't know," Grant remarked, "but this is turning into one strange place!"

The roar of an approaching boat engine **penetrated** the sounds of the crashing waves and gusty wind. A powerful beam of light passed over the *Mystery Girl*. Papa, Christina, and Grant had to cover their eyes.

"This is the U.S. Coast Guard. Is everybody okay?" a booming voice shouted through a bullhorn.

"We're here!" Christina and Grant shouted. "We're okay!"

"We're coming ashore," the bullhorn voice said. "Stay where you are!"

"Ha!" Grant said, looking at Papa and spreading his arms with his palms facing up to the sky. "Where are we going to go?"

Papa broke out in laughter and then winced from the pain in his ankle.

Christina noticed that Mimi had barely gotten the word 'Mayday' out of her mouth before the Coast Guard showed up. *How did they know we were here? How did they find us? And what was that crazy bird squawking about? What are we going to see clearly? This mystery was heating up!*

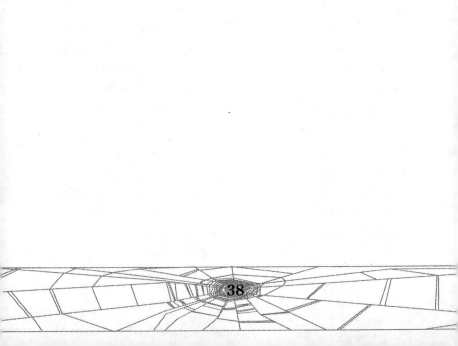

5
I WANT BLACK!
BUT PINK IS PRETTIER!

The Coast Guard cutter rounded the Hatteras Inlet into Pamlico Sound as it headed south toward a hospital in Morehead City. Mimi closely watched everything the Coast Guard emergency medical technician did for Papa.

Papa rested comfortably with his foot raised on a rolled-up blanket.

"I think it should be pink," she said, stroking Papa's head. "When I broke my leg as a little girl, they only had white casts. I've always wanted to get a pink cast if I ever broke my leg again."

"Well," Papa said, "the next time you break your leg, you can get a pink cast, but I'm getting a black cast. That way, no one can sign the silly thing."

"Hmm!" Mimi said. "They do make glow pens that write on black surfaces, so your plan may not work! If you're okay, I'm going to check on the kids."

"I'm in great hands," Papa said, nodding at the EMT. "While you're up there, see if you can find out who we call to get the *Mystery Girl* off that sandbar tomorrow, weather permitting."

Mimi nodded as she moved toward the front of the boat, holding the rail for stability.

Grant and Christina were in the boat's pilothouse talking to a lieutenant when Mimi joined them.

"Isn't this boat awesome, Mimi?" Grant asked.

"Yes, Grant," Mimi said, "but I do believe this is one of the Coast Guard's smaller boats."

"Your grandmother's right," the lieutenant said. "We have one really cool, historic sailing ship you might want to see called the *Barque Eagle*. She's in port at Morehead City." The lieutenant handed Mimi a card. "If you want a tour, I can set one up for you."

Grant jumped up and down. "Can we, Mimi?" he said. "I'd love to see an old sailing ship!"

"I don't see why not," Mimi said, scanning the card. "Uh, Lieutenant Bailey, how did you find us so quickly?"

"We received an anonymous emergency radio call with your coordinates," the lieutenant replied. "We headed out as soon as we got the call."

Mimi peered at Grant over her red reading glasses decorated with sparkly rhinestones. "Maybe we did have an angel after all!" she remarked.

"You just might have," Lieutenant Bailey said. "For the last 50 to 60 years, we've gotten an anonymous emergency rescue call in almost every major storm we've had. They've always been from the same guy too, except maybe during the first five or six years. I heard those calls sounded like a girl."

"You're joking," Mimi said. "I was teasing about the angel."

"No," Lieutenant Bailey said. "I'm serious. We've never been able to identify who he is, so we just call him our OBA, or Outer Banks Angel. I can't count how many lives he's responsible for saving over the years. He deserves a medal for every one of them!"

"Wow, that's cool," Grant exclaimed. "A real live angel!"

Mimi suddenly remembered Papa's request. "Do you know someone who can help get our plane off the sandbar tomorrow?" she asked.

"I do," Lieutenant Bailey answered, pulling another card from his wallet.

Christina and Grant moved over to the starboard, or right side, of the boat. "What do you think?" Christina said.

"What do I think about what?" Grant asked.

"About tonight, about the angel, about that crazy bird!" Christina said.

Grant shrugged. "I don't know for sure," he remarked. "I do think we might have had an angel help us, but I don't know what that bird was trying to say."

The Coast Guard boat pulled alongside a sturdy wooden dock. An ambulance waited on the pier, its lights glistening off of the slick wet buildings along the shoreline.

Christina repeated the bird's clue. "Survive the shoals, and you'll see it clearly," she said. "Maybe it's a clue to something."

"I guess," Grant said. "Or maybe it's just a crazy bird."

Christina shook her head. "No," she said. "There's more to this. I just have a feeling."

"Well, if it's a clue," Grant said, wiping more sweat off his forehead, "you'll have lots of time to figure it out at the hospital. If their hospitals are anything like ours, we'll be spending most of the night there."

6
WHAT A DIFFERENCE!

Grant was right, Christina thought, peering out the window at the late morning sun. They'd spent most of the night in the hospital emergency room while the doctor examined Papa and put a black cast on his broken ankle.

A taxi dropped them off at their rental house on Cape Hatteras around five in the morning. Christina had been in and out of sleep since then.

Christina slid out from the lower bunk bed. She saw that Grant was already dressed and gone. Where did he go, she wondered.

After getting dressed, Christina searched the house, but couldn't find anyone. She poured a bowl of cereal and tiptoed out to the deck.

"There you are!" she said, seeing Papa and Mimi relaxing in deck chairs. Grant was perched on the deck railing up against the side of the house. A fan above them turned at a leisurely pace, as if the heat sapped its energy too.

"Good morning, young lady," Papa said. "We wondered when you'd finally get up."

"We were afraid you might sleep the day away!" Mimi added, taking a sip of pink lemonade from a tall glass with green frogs painted on it.

"Sleep!" Christina almost chuckled. "How can anyone sleep in this heat?"

"Mimi says it's not really that hot," Grant said. "It's just the high humid...humdid...how do you say that, Mimi?"

"Humidity," Mimi said with a laugh. "You feel warmer in a humid climate like this."

"Either way," Christina remarked, "I don't understand how people can live here."

"That's simple," Papa said, motioning toward the ocean.

The sky was a beautiful azure blue, dotted with milky white, cotton-candy clouds. The ocean was calm and a deeper blue than the sky above. Gentle waves rolled up onto the beach.

"Wow!" Christina said. "What a difference a night makes."

"Yep," Grant said. "It's beautiful all right, but other than going swimming, there doesn't seem to be much to do around here."

Mimi spotted a young man walking along the beach. He waved as he headed toward them.

"Who's that?" Christina asked.

"Oh, I'll bet that's Sean," Mimi said. "He lives a few doors down. We're renting this beach house from his parents. His mom told me she would send him over to meet us."

"Why?" Christina asked.

"To show you and Grant around the area," Mimi replied. She rose from her seat. "Hi! You must be Sean!"

The smiling boy was a head taller than Christina and a couple of years older. He had a deep tan and short, brownish-blonde hair. He sauntered up the stairs to the deck, which like the rest of the house, was raised on stilts to protect it from high tides and storms.

Sean introduced himself and shook everyone's hands. He explained that he had lived on the North Carolina coast all his life.

"So, I guess you know this island pretty well," Mimi said.

The boy chuckled. "I know the North Carolina coastline better than the back of my hand," he said.

"Great!" Mimi said. "Do you have time to show my grandchildren around the area?"

"Sure," Sean answered. "I hope they like hanging out on the beach!"

Grant slipped off the railing and pressed his back against what he thought was the wall.

"Grant," Papa said. "Be careful there, you're leaning against the laundry chute!"

"AAAAHHHHHH!"

Grant screamed as he fell backwards through the laundry chute door. He tumbled down the chute and flew into the laundry room.

CLUNK!
WHAM!

Grant landed right on top of the big white clothes dryer. Sean leaped down the deck steps to check on him. Grant was lying on the dryer, rubbing his sore bottom.

Sean began to laugh. "So, did you dent the dryer?" he asked.

Grant's pained expression dissolved into giggles. "I don't know, but I sure dented my bottom!" he cried.

"I can see you and I are going to have a lot of fun!" Sean said.

7
A SCOTCH BONNET

Sean, Christina, and Grant walked down the beach in silence until Grant spotted a perfectly shaped seashell. "Hey," Grant said, "look at this!" He scooped up the shell and twirled it around.

Sean leaned over and peered intently at the shell. "That's a Scotch Bonnet," he said. "It's the North Carolina state shell!"

Christina looked closely at it. "How can you tell?" she asked.

"It's easy," Sean said. "See these spiral grooves? On a Scotch Bonnet, there are usually twenty of them. Plus, the creamy white color and yellowish brown squares kind of give it away. This is about as big as they get, around four inches. It's a keeper!"

"How do you know so much about seashells?" Grant asked.

"I grew up here, so learning about shells is second nature," Sean said. "You just kind of automatically become a seashell collector."

"Is it always this easy to find cool shells?" Grant asked.

"No," Sean said, "but the best time for shelling is after a storm like we had last night. I have an awesome shell collection."

Grant held out his shell. "Would you like this one?" he asked.

"No," Sean said. "I already have several like that in my collection. I'm looking for a Giant Tun shell. It has a very thin shell, so it's hard to find a perfect whole one."

Grant pointed over Sean's shoulder. "Hey, check out that lighthouse!"

"It's so cool," Sean said. "It's the most photographed lighthouse in America."

"I can see why," Christina said. "It looks like one of those poles you see in an old barber shop—like the one where Papa gets his hair cut."

As they worked their way toward the lighthouse, Grant was about to grab a purple, spiral-shaped shell when he suddenly stopped. "Do you hear that?" he asked.

"Hear what?" Sean said.

"The bird," Grant said, turning to Christina. "It's the bird from last night!"

SQUAWK! SQUAWK!

The majestic Macaw parrot flew toward Grant, its wings whipping through the muggy air. Grant stuck out his arm, and the parrot landed on it.

The beasts can't stop you, but they make you weary.

The parrot swung his head back and forth as it gazed into one of Grant's eyes and then the other. "The beasts can't stop you, but they make you weary," it repeated again.

"That's weird," Sean said. "Do you always attract birds?"

SQUAWK!

The bird flapped its yellow wings and soared down the beach.

"No," Grant said. "I don't know why that bird likes me."

Christina tilted her head to the side. "The beasts can't stop you, but they make you weary," she repeated.

"You mean you've met this bird before?" Sean asked.

"Yes!" Grant said. "He landed on our plane after our emergency landing last night." Grant told him what happened.

"What did it say last night?" Sean asked.

Grant pointed to Christina. "I don't remember exactly," he said. "Christina's the one with the great memory."

Sean spun around toward Christina. "So," he said. "What did it say?"

"Let's see," Christina said, looking skyward, "it said, 'Survive the shoals, and you'll see it clearly'."

"Hmm!" Sean said. "That makes just about as much sense as what it just said. I don't get either of them, but I'm bad with riddles. Sometimes I don't even get knock, knock jokes."

"Riddles!" Christina said. "That's what it's doing!"

"What?" Grant said. "What's it doing?"

"I think it's giving us pieces of a riddle," Christina said. "'Survive the shoals, and you'll see it clearly. The beasts can't stop you, but they make you weary.' See, it's part of a riddle."

"Okay, but it still doesn't make any sense," Grant said, turning to Sean. "You're really not good at knock, knock jokes?"

"Nope," Sean said. "Not at all."

"Knock, knock!" Grant said.

Sean shook his head. "Who's there?"

"Macaw!" Grant said.

"Macaw who?" Sean answered.

"Ma cawed you last night, but you didn't answer," Grant said, laughing.

Sean scratched his head. "I don't get it."

"Wow!" Grant said. "You are bad with knock, knock jokes!"

A loud, raspy voice interrupted Grant's joke telling. "WHAT ARE YOU DOING HERE?"

The children spun around to face a rail-thin man with a gray scraggly beard. His face was deeply furrowed, like muddy ruts alongside a road. His clothes were tattered, especially his pants, which were ripped off into shorts that rested just above his knobby knees.

"This is my beach!" he yelled, pointing to a makeshift shelter he had built among a group of boulders and a couple of scrawny trees. A tattered boat rested next to the shelter.

"You get out of here right now!" he said. "I don't like uninvited guests, and I especially don't like children taking my shells.

"SHOO!" he said. "SHOO!" He made a motion like he was shooing away birds.

"Okay, Mister M," Sean said. "We're going. We don't want any trouble." Sean turned. "Come on, let's get out of here, before he does something weird."

"But I thought the beach was public property," Grant said.

"It is," Sean said, "but I'm not going to argue with him. Do you want to?"

Grant looked back at the man. He stood there with his hands on his hips, glaring at them.

"No," Grant said. "That guy gives me the creeps!"

Christina, Grant, and Sean turned and raced to the lighthouse.

Christina's mind was racing as she ran. *Where did that parrot come from? What do the pieces of the riddle mean? She had to find out!*

8

STAIR CLIMBING, ANYONE?

Grant plopped down on a bench outside the lighthouse entrance and glared at Sean. "You're not even sweating or breathing hard," Grant said, inhaling as much air as he could while wiping the sweat off his face with his shirt.

"I've grown up here," Sean said, "so I'm **acclimated** to the thick air. At least that's what my dad says. He's the Cape Hatteras lighthouse keeper."

"Whoa, really?" Grant said, tilting his head back and looking up toward the top of the lighthouse. "That's cool. Where's the elevator to the top?"

Sean laughed. "Come on, I'll show you," he said. He motioned for the kids to follow him.

When they stepped into the lighthouse, Sean pointed toward the staircase that led out of sight. "Here's the elevator!"

"Very funny!" Christina said.

"Come on!" he urged. "I'll tell you the history of the lighthouse as we climb. There's only 268 stairs."

"Wait a minute," Grant said. "You want to climb these stairs all the way to the top? Are you crazy?"

"No!" Sean said. "I climb them at least once a day."

"Well," Grant said, "I guess that explains why you're not breathing hard."

Sean stepped up the stairs as he talked. Christina and Grant followed. "Believe it or not," he began, "the Cape Hatteras Lighthouse is 208 feet tall. It's the tallest lighthouse in America.

"Lighthouses were built along the Outer Banks to warn ships of the shallow sandbars of Diamond Shoals, which reach 14 miles out into the ocean," Sean said. "But they weren't very effective because their dim lights didn't penetrate the fog or darkness very well. Around 1850, everything changed. The Fresnel lens was invented, allowing lighthouses to be seen far out at sea."

"Fresnel lens?" Christina said.

"Yep," Sean said. "It was developed in France by a guy named—"

"Fresnel, I'll bet," Grant said.

How many more stairs do I have to climb?

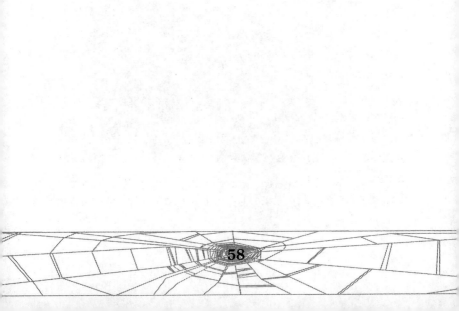

58

"You got it!" Sean replied. "It used prisms and magnifying glasses to increase the light from a small whale oil lamp into a powerful beacon. The light beacon could be seen 20 to 50 miles out at sea, depending on the weather."

Sean reached the 75th step and looked back at Christina and Grant. They were both breathing pretty hard. "Do you want to take a break?"

"Not yet," gasped Christina.

"Okay," Sean said, as he continued to walk and talk. "This is the second Cape Hatteras lighthouse. The first one, which had a stationary light, was in bad shape after the Civil War, so they decided to build a taller and better one.

"This one had a rotating beacon," Sean continued, "which my great, great grandfather had to rewind every 12 hours. It used a weight that descended slowly from the top of the tower down to the base, along with a series of gears to turn the beacon."

"Does it still use a whale oil lamp today?" Grant asked.

"No," Sean said. "Now it uses two 1000-watt lamps. The lighthouse was supposed to be painted in a diamond pattern so it could be seen easily during the day as a landmark for ships. But the guy that painted it got the painting plans mixed up with Cape Lookout's lighthouse, which is just down the coast. Cape Lookout ended up with the diamond pattern and Cape Hatteras got the spiral striping Cape Lookout was supposed to get. This lighthouse is called the 'Big Barber Pole' because of the stripes."

Sean started to breathe heavier, as he passed the 125th step. "We're almost halfway there. Do you want to rest?"

"No," Grant mumbled. "Not until you're breathing as heavy as we are. Why do you climb this thing every day, anyway?" Grant asked.

"It's kind of my special place," Sean said. "I love the view and it's where I can get away from everything and think."

"How can it be special if anybody can climb up here?" Christina asked, pulling herself up to the 150th step.

"Surprisingly," Sean replied, "very few people make it to the top. Most of them turn around less than halfway up."

"We're the winners!" Grant cried. "But I think it's time to take a break."

They all sat down on a stair. "Is the lighthouse still in use?" Christina asked. "I think it would be outdated with the new GPS **navigation** aids."

"Yes," Sean said, "it's still used, but more as a landmark. Everything still works, though. It's just done with electricity and motors now. Like you said, ships today have advanced equipment to get them around the shoals. But even with that, there's still an occasional shipwreck."

Grant stood up and took a deep breath. "Okay, let's get this over with," he said.

When they finally reached the top, Grant collapsed against the window looking out to sea. "Whew!" he said, panting hard. "I don't believe it. I made it!"

Christina was already taking in the view. "You're right," she said, gulping in deep breaths. "This is incredible! What's that over there?"

"It's the last shipwreck we had," Sean said. "It happened in a storm about six months ago. There were six people onboard when it ran aground. After the Coast Guard saved them, they found out the OBA had radioed in their exact position to the Coast Guard."

"OBA!" Grant said. "You mean the Outer Banks Angel?"

"Yeah!" Sean said. "You've heard of him?"

"Yep!" Christina said. Her breathing was starting to settle down. "We think he was responsible for rescuing us too."

"They say no one knows who he is," Grant said. "Is that true?"

"Well, we just know he's an angel who helps out people in distress," Sean said. He spun around to face the kids. "If you like to talk about shipwrecks, let me show you this great map of shipwrecks," he added, walking around to the other side of the lighthouse.

Christina followed him. "Come on, Grant!" she bellowed, seeing him still leaning up against the window, gasping for air. *Maybe I'll find some clues to this mysterious parrot and mysterious angel in this lighthouse, she thought. It's worth a try!*

9
SHIPWRECKS GALORE!

"There have been more than 500 shipwrecks along the banks, from the Virginia border down to Cape Lookout, roughly about 175 miles," Sean said. "This map shows some of the major shipwrecks, like the *Monitor*, the *Patriot*, and the *Enterprize*."

Grant and Christina crowded around the wrinkled, yellowed map on the wall. "Papa told me that Mimi had a map like this," Grant said, looking at all the shipwrecks and reading the little tags telling of their fates. "Wow," he added, "some of these stories are really sad."

"But look at this one about the *Enterprize*," Christina remarked. "In 1822, the ship ran aground about 30 miles north of this lighthouse. The ship began to take on water, and they couldn't tell how far they were from shore in the dark. There was a horse on board the ship, and the crew decided to push it overboard! They figured if the horse made it to land, they could too!"

"What happened?" Grant asked, wide-eyed.

"It was shallow enough that the horse just about waded to shore!" Christina exclaimed. "All of the passengers and crew just followed him!"

"Wow!" Grant replied. "Saved by a horse!"

As Grant continued to scour the shipwreck map, Christina gazed out the window. They were on the south side of the lighthouse facing the southern shoreline. She finally spotted the house Mimi and Papa had rented a mile down the beach, but couldn't see if they were on the deck.

"Hey, Sean," Christina asked, "do you have a pair of binoculars up here?"

Sean smiled. "Of course," he replied, stepping over to a cabinet with a combination lock. He quickly opened it and pulled out the binoculars. "Here you go," he said.

Christina looked down the shore again. "Just as I thought—Papa's sitting on the deck, reading a book. But then again, it's possible he's sleeping with a book on his lap. It's hard to tell."

"Let me see," Grant said, taking the binoculars from Christina. "Yep," he said. "He's sleeping. I can tell by the position of his head." He handed the binoculars back to Christina.

Christina looked through them again. This time, she moved the binoculars up the beach back toward the lighthouse. She stopped, catching a glimpse of the old man who'd chased them away earlier.

"Hey," Christina said, "I see the old man. Sean, didn't you call him Mister M? What do you know about him?"

"Not much," Sean said. "I don't think anyone does. My dad says he's lived on the beach since before he was born. People say he's a grouchy hermit and from my experience with him, they're right. He rarely talks to anyone. He just fishes, sleeps, and moves about the island. Sometimes he goes out in that rickety boat of his, but that's all I know."

"Why does everyone call him 'Mister M'?" Christina asked.

"I don't know," Sean said, shrugging his shoulders. "They just do. My dad calls him 'Double M.' I never asked him why."

Christina looked through the binoculars again. *A shiver ran down her spine as she saw the old man looking back at her with a scowl on his face.*

10
THE HAUNTING

Sean, Christina, and Grant worked their way down the stairs and were about to leave when someone called Sean's name.

"Sean! Sean! What are you doing?" the voice yelled. It belonged to a young African American girl.

Sean smiled. "Sally," he said. "it's about time you got back from your grandma's house."

"I know," Sally said. "We just got back yesterday, in time for tonight's annual crab boil." She took off her Boston Red Sox hat and smiled at the kids.

"Great!" Sean said. "Sally, this is Christina and Grant. They're from Georgia."

"What's a crab boil?" Grant asked, following Sean around the lighthouse. "Why would someone boil a crab?"

"To eat it!" Sean replied. "Sally is the great, great granddaughter of one of the early black lifesavers from Pea Island, north of here. Every year the descendants of the lifesavers get together for a crab boil and the oldest members tell stories about the lifesavers' adventures."

"Yeah!" Sally said. "You guys ought to come. Sean comes every year."

"I'm not sure our grandparents will let us," Christina said.

"Bring them!" Sally offered. "We have plenty of food! As my mama says, the more that come, the less she has to take home with her."

"Do they eat the claws?" asked Grant, still concerned about boiling crabs.

"No, you pull delicious meat out of them," Sally said. "You'll see; it tastes really good!"

"Hey, follow me," Sean said. The kids walked to the back of the lighthouse and Sean looked around to make sure no one was watching them. "There's something else Sally and I do every year, just before school starts," he whispered.

"What's that?" Grant asked.

Sean grabbed the handle to a door with a sign on it that said 'Utility Room.' "Sally and I think the lighthouse is haunted!"

"Really?" Christina said.

"Yeah!" Sean said. "A few years back, Sally and I were in this utility room and saw a ghost. Every year we come back to see if the ghost is still here."

"Yeah!" Sally added. "Years ago, a sailboat, with a newlywed couple onboard, went down in high waves 100 yards offshore from the lighthouse. They never found them. But we think her spirit haunts the lighthouse as she waits for her husband to come ashore because she's always there, wearing a bride's dress."

"You're crazy," Grant said. "There's no such thing as ghosts."

"Really!" Sean said. "Didn't you say earlier that you saw a ghost the night you arrived?"

"Yes, but—" Grant started.

"No buts!" Sean said. "A ghost is a ghost. Come on, follow me." Sean turned the door handle. "Sally, you bring up the rear."

Sean pulled on a string hanging from a dim 25-watt bulb inside the doorway. The light cast a faint glow in the dark room.

"Why come here every year, if you know there's a ghost in here?" Christina asked.

Sean shrugged. "I guess each year we convince ourselves there is no ghost, so we come back to prove it again."

They crept toward the back of the utility room. "I don't see anything!" Grant whispered.

A brisk wind blew past them. The light went out and the utility door slammed shut.

"What's going on?" Christina squealed.

"I think it's near...nearby," Sean said, his voice shaking. "The door's never shut before. Grant, see...see if you can open it."

"I would, but I can't see where it is," Grant said. "Maybe Sall—"

Along the back wall, a vertical beam of soft light appeared. It slowly grew in intensity. It looked like a wedding dress swaying gently back and forth.
"It's the ghost!" Grant screamed, as he ran to the door, which he could now see in the soft glow from the ghost's light. He turned the door handle and pushed, but it wouldn't budge. "It's stuck!" he shouted.

Christina and Sean pushed on the door, screaming along with Grant. The ghost seemed to move toward them. "Come on!" Christina shouted. "We've got to get out of here! Push harder!"

Suddenly, the door flew open. Grant and Christina burst from the room, as if they had

Help! Get us out of here!

exploded from a cannon. They ran several yards until they heard Sean and Sally howling with laughter.

Grant turned to his sister. "They tricked us!" Grant shouted. "That's no fair!"

After Sean and Sally were down to just giggles, Christina said, "Okay, how did you do it?"

"We really didn't do much," Sean said, walking around the front of the lighthouse. "We held off taking you into the utility room until I saw people heading to the lighthouse's main door. When we entered, I knew it wouldn't be long before the people opened the door. When that door opens, it creates a strong breeze through the utility room."

Sean smiled and looked at Sally. "And that's when I turned off the light, ran out, and shut and locked the door from the outside," Sally added.

"Okay," Christina said. "But how did you create the ghost?"

"We didn't," Sean said. "After locking the door, Sally ran up to the main door and opened it again. But this time, she opened it all the way. It closes very slowly. The light coming through the door passes through two floor registers, which circulate air throughout the lighthouse. The registers split the light up and reflect it on the utility room's back wall. As the door slowly closes, it creates shadows—"

"Which look like a ghost in a bride's dress!" Sally interrupted. "That's why we made up the story about the shipwreck."

"That was pretty good," Grant said. "You scared me, but that was still a good trick!"

11

IN HOT WATER!

"You've got to try it," Sean said.

"I don't know," Grant replied. "It looks like a big, slimy booger!"

"Okay," Sean said. "You're right about that, but haven't you ever tried something that looked bad, but tasted really good?"

"Not that I can think of," Grant mumbled. His eyes fell on Papa about five seats down from him and across the table. He watched Papa scoop up an oyster and dump it down his throat. Papa smiled at him.

"Okay," Grant said. "I'll give it a shot." He held the oyster over his mouth and tilted his head back. All I've got to do is swallow it quickly, he thought. He dumped it into his mouth, tried to swallow, but couldn't. The salty, fishy taste was too much. He quickly spit it out.

"YUCK!" Grant cried, gulping down some fruit juice. "That's nasty! How could Papa eat those?" He looked at Papa, still smiling at him. The oyster shell was still in his hand. He turned it so Grant could see that his finger was pressing the oyster into the shell. He had never swallowed it!

Sean, Sally, Christina, and Mimi were laughing. "Gotcha!" Mimi said.

Grant frowned. "That's not funny," he said. "That nasty taste is still in my mouth! And I can't believe I fell for that old trick."

"What's that?" Christina asked, balancing her plate on her lap. She pulled a bit of crab out of the shell, dipped it in butter, and tossed it in her mouth.

"The art of diversion," Grant said. "Making someone think you're doing something that you're not. Every magician does it. Do you eat those nasty things, Sally?"

Grant decided it was his turn to play a trick. Once Christina turned her head toward Sally, Grant reached in a bag next to the big aluminum crab pot and pulled out a live crab. He quickly replaced the cooked crab on Christina's plate with the live crab.

"Are you crazy?" Sally said, sticking her nose in the air. "I've got more culture than that."

Seafood, anyone?

Christina laughed. Without looking, she reached for another piece of crab. When her fingers touched the crab, it scurried off her plate!

"AAAAAHHHHHH!"

Christina screamed.

Everyone around her burst into laughter.

"Grant!" Christina yelled. "I'm going to get you!" She tried to punch Grant in the arm, but missed him as he danced down the beach.

12
COAST GUARD TO THE RESCUE

After dinner, everyone at the crab boil gathered around the bonfire. The humid air felt less sticky in the early evening hours. Christina settled down next to Sean. She felt comforted by the sound of the frothy white waves lapping at the shore. This place was very different from her home in Georgia, Christina thought, but she was beginning to like it.

Grant plopped in the sand next to his sister. He had enjoyed every bite of his dinner, except for that oyster, of course! He told Mimi his buttery corn on the cob was the best he'd ever eaten, and still had greasy butter stains on his red cheeks.

Christina noticed Sally standing next to an old black man in a blue-and-white striped beach chair. That must be Old Man Billy, her great granddaddy, Christina thought.

The old black man's face was withered like an aged piece of leather. He cleared his throat and began to speak.

"My pappy was named Richard Etheridge," he began. Christina was surprised at his deep, lyrical voice. The dark night seemed to swallow his small stature, but the firelight illuminated the spark of emotion in his eyes.

Old Man Billy smiled at Sally and took her hand. "It was 1880," he continued, "when my pappy became the first black keeper in the U.S. Lifesaving Service at the Pea Island station. But no white lifesaver, or surfman, wanted to serve under a black keeper. So they left, and black surfmen took their place. My pappy went through tough times fighting not only the sea, but also the **prejudice** of the times. He was a proud man and a hard worker, so he fought on."

Old Man Billy looked at Grant. "Pappy trained his men to be the best they could be," he continued. "Each day was set aside for learning a different duty.

"On Monday, he built their strength by having them drag the heavy surfboat through the sand by hand. On Tuesday, they cleaned the station and repaired and polished equipment. On Wednesday, they practiced signal flags. On Thursday, they performed drills with their rescue equipment. Friday was the day to practice first aid and resuscitation methods. Saturday was for doing laundry and cleaning personal gear. Sunday was saved as a day of rest and a day of worship."

Sally handed Old Man Billy a cup of water. He took a swallow and cleared his throat. "My pappy didn't stop with teaching his men their jobs," he continued. "He also taught them to read and to write so they could pass a special test to become government employees.

"But Pappy knew," he said, "that the most important thing was saving lives. So his crew kept watch. Sunshine or rain, they signaled ships with warnings of the hazards of the shoals. They'd walk the beach halfway to the next lifesaving station in each direction and exchange tokens with that station's lifesaver to prove they'd each completed their patrols."

Old Man Billy shifted in his seat. "My pappy led the rescues and steered the surfboat. He believed in the service's motto, *You have to go out and that's a fact. But nothing says you have to come back.*"

Grant and Christina were mesmerized by Old Man Billy's story. "But there comes a day in every man's life that tests what he's made of," he continued, his voice getting louder. "That day came for Pappy's men on October 11, 1896, during the worst storm of the century. It was a terrible storm— a beast.

"Pappy knew there was no way he could use the Breeches buoy—"

Grant interrupted the old man. "What's that?" he asked, hanging on every word of the story.

"Young man," Old Man Billy said, "the Breeches buoy was a rescue device that used a pair of canvas shorts sewn to a lifesaving ring. The rescuers would shoot a pulley line with the Breeches buoy attached out to the ship with a special cannon. After it was tied off to the mast, the person hung in the Breeches buoy, dangling over the ocean. The surfmen pulled the person inch-by-inch to safety on the beach."

The old man smiled at Grant and nodded.

"Please go on," Christina pleaded.

"So," Old Man Billy said, "most folks would have thought there was no chance of rescuing the captain, his wife, their three-year-old son, and the crew of the E.S. Newman schooner in that beast of a storm. Its sails were torn off in the hurricane, and the captain decided to beach it before he lost her to the sea.

"That didn't stop Pappy, though," Old Man Billy added. "He knew he had to try. He told his men to tie a heavy line around two of the surfmen. They took an extra line and swam out to the boat through the roughest seas they'd ever seen. The fact they reached the boat proved Pappy's training was worth the sweat and tears."

Old Man Billy swallowed another sip of water. "When they climbed onboard," he continued, "the captain tied his three-year old son to one of the surfmen, who struggled back to shore and saved the child's life. Pappy's crew took turns going out to rescue the rest of the crew. It took six hours to rescue all nine people and bring them to shore one by one, but they did it!"

"Wow!" Grant said. "They were brave!"

"You are right, son," Old Man Billy said. "In the 69 years the Pea Island station operated, its crews saved 600 lives, more than any other station in the history of the Lifesaving Service. And in 1915, the Lifesaving Service and the Revenue Cutter Service merged to become the U.S. Coast Guard, the water rescuers of today.

"But it wasn't until nearly 100 years later," Old Man Billy added, "that Pappy and the Pea Island Station crew finally received the recognition they deserved. They were awarded the Gold Lifesaving Medal for their heroics in the rescue of the crew of the *E.S. Newman*.

"And that's why we have this annual crab boil," Old Man Billy said, scanning the young eyes in front of him and stopping at Grant, "so we can pass on Pappy's way of looking at life. Work hard and dedicate yourself to something that matters in life!"

Christina's mind wandered back to something Old Man Billy had said. He called the storm a 'beast,' she thought. *Were storms the beasts that made you weary?*

13
PERMISSION GRANTED

Grant rose early the next morning. Mimi found him sitting on the deck facing the ocean, staring out to sea. "You're up awfully early," she said, tying her red robe around her waist.

"I'm the early bird catching the worm!" he replied. Mimi laughed and wrapped Grant in a big bear hug.

"What do you kids have planned for today?" she asked, just as Christina walked out the door onto the deck already dressed and ready for the day.

"Remember how you told me you used to go out on the ocean with the rowboat, but that I was too young to do that?" Christina asked.

"Yes, I do," Mimi said. "Why do you ask?"

"Well," Christina answered, "Sean is just a little older than me, and he has rowed boats all around

Cape Hatteras. So, can we go with Sean and Sally out to a sandbar that has a shipwreck on it?"

Mimi sat quietly for several seconds. She peered at Christina and Grant over her multicolored reading glasses with little rhinestones on the edges. "I tell you what," she said, "I'll let you go, but you have to promise to keep your life vests on at all times and to check in with me every hour. Understood?"

"Yes, yes!" Christina said. "I'll take my cell phone!"

"Remember, every hour on the hour, or I call in the Coast Guard," Mimi warned.

"I can fix that," Grant said, taking the phone from Christina. He ran his fingers expertly over the keyboard. "There, I've set the alarm to go off every hour, so we don't forget."

Christina and Grant kissed Mimi and rushed down the beach to meet Sean and Sally.

SQUEEEEEAAAAKKKK!

Papa used his crutch to push open the creaky screen door. "You kids be careful!" he called after them.

Christina whirled around, a big grin on her face. "We will, Papa!" she cried. "We will!"

14

ROW, ROW, ROW YOUR BOAT

Grant pulled on the oar with all his might. "No!" he called, giggling. "Paddle the other direction." As soon as Sean started paddling the other direction, Grant changed the direction he was paddling, so they kept spinning the boat in circles.

"Boys!" Christina exclaimed. "Can you please stop fooling around? The people on the beach are beginning to stare at us."

"But this is fun," Sean said, as they spun the boat in the other direction.

"Oh! I feel like I'm going to be sick," Sally warned, standing over the two boys pretending like she was ready to throw up.

"Okay! Okay!" Sean said. "We get the point."

Sean took the other oar from Grant and paddled toward the sandbar. He quickly built up a steady, strong stroke in the mild surf.

Grant pounded the wooden seat, shouting, "Stroke! Stroke! Stroke!" to Sean's rhythmic motion.

The boat zigzagged through the maze of sandbars as Sean tried to find his way to the shipwreck. After fifteen minutes, Sally looked back at the beach. They hadn't made much progress. "What's the problem, Sean?" she asked. "We should have been there by now."

"The last storm changed everything around," Sean said. "Sandbars have disappeared, only to be replaced by other ones in different places. I'm having to plot a new course."

"It's a sandbar maze," Grant observed, "and we're the rats trying to find our way through it!"

Sean pulled around a small sandbar. It looked like he had a clear shot through the water to the shipwreck. "Okay," he said. "I think I've got it."

"That ship looks a lot bigger the closer we get to it," Christina said.

"It should," Sean said, in between taking deep breaths. "It's a 60-foot sailboat. It doesn't look like much now, but it used to have beautiful teak decking with polished brass rails. I saw it before people started plundering it."

"Plundering it?" Grant asked.

"Yep!" Sally said. "Once people see an abandoned boat, they start taking everything they can from it. Everything on a boat is worth money, the brass, the teakwood, engines, instruments, and even the furnishings."

Sean gave the oars several extra strong strokes to wedge the small boat onto the sand.

Grant was about to jump out when Sean grabbed his arm. "Whoa!" he ordered. "Never jump out of a boat before making sure there are no jellyfish or anything else you might step on," he said. "You don't want to get a nasty surprise!"

Grant nodded and peeked over the boat's side. The water and sand were clear. They scurried across the sandbar to the wreck, which was tilted slightly on its side.

"This is cool!" Grant said, climbing up to the main deck. He stood where the helm had been before someone stole it. He pretended he was the helmsman. "Hey, ye maties, where you be wantin' to go?" Grant twisted the imaginary wheel back and forth.

"Sir," Christina said, pretending to flap a hand fan like a Victorian woman. "You must take us to London. My fiancé has a business there, and I really must see him before I faint from this heat."

Sally ran up to Grant. "No, sir," she said. "You simply must take us to the Orient. I hear the tea is exquisite and the silk dresses are extraordinary."

Sean snatched a long stick from the deck and whipped it from side to side. "Listen here, matey," he said, "You'll be sorry if you don't yield to my command. I'm takin' over this ship!"

Grant giggled as he took a step back from the imaginary helm. "You'd make a good pirate!" he said.

CRACK!

The old, withered deck boards underneath Grant gave way. He disappeared!

15

SHIPWRECK TREASURE

PLOP!

Grant plunged through the deck onto a thick pile of sand, and landed right on his bottom. It had happened so fast he didn't have time to scream.

He didn't hurt himself, but his left wrist was a little sore. "Why does this keep happening?" he asked no one in particular. "I've got to be more careful!"

Christina raced down the stairs into the cabin where Grant had fallen. "Grant!" she called. "Are you okay?" Sean and Sally followed close behind.

"I'm good," Grant said, flexing his wrist back and forth. "It'll take more than a little fall to stop me, Captain Grant! I was planning to come down here anyway to see if there was any hidden treasure. I just got here a little faster than I'd planned!"

Ring! Ring! Ring!

Christina jumped. "Relax, Christina," Grant said. "It's just the cell phone alarm telling us it's time to call Mimi."

Grant reached down to push himself up. His hand settled into the deep pile of sand that had washed into the cabin. His fingers touched something smooth.

"What's this?" Grant said, lifting his find up into the light beam coming through the hole he'd made in the deck above.

"Wow!" Sean said. "That looks like a Giant Tun shell! Let me see it!"

"It sure does," Sally said.

Grant twirled it around in his hand. "It's definitely a shell," he said, handing it to Sean.

Sean looked it over. "It's a perfect Giant Tun shell," he said. "There are no chips or unwanted markings. This thing is priceless, at least to a shell collector!"

"You actually found a treasure, Grant," Christina said, pressing the speed dial number for Mimi's cell phone. "You're the only person I know who could fall through something, not get hurt, and then walk away with a treasure."

Grant flexed his bicep muscles. "Oh, yeah, oh, yeah," he bragged. He motioned toward the shell. "I may have found the treasure, but Sean's the collector, so he gets to keep it." He scowled and began speaking like a pirate. "Now, if it were gold, me matey," he said, "you would have to fight me for it!"

"Are you sure?" Sean asked. "Adding this to your other shell would give you a start to a great collection."

"I'm sure," Grant said, turning around and digging through the sand with his hands. "I wonder if there's any buried gold down here."

Christina closed the phone and dropped to the sand next to Grant. "Mimi said she's glad we're having fun and that you should be careful."

"You didn't tell her..." Grant started.

"...that you fell?" Christina interrupted. "No! She just knows you, that's all. Now it's my turn to find some treasure," she said, digging her hands into the sand.

Christina's hand brushed over something. Another shell, she thought. "I've got something!" she said, as she pulled her discovery out of the sand and held it up to her face. She saw her reflection looking back at her.

"It's a hand mirror!" Sally said. "And it's really old!"

Christina scanned the fine scrolled edges of the mirror. They were light blue and silver. The glass was cracked and stained. "It's beautiful," she said. "It must have belonged to someone in a shipwreck!"

"That's pretty cool," Grant said. "Look! It has someone's initials on it."

"It does?" Christina said, flipping over the mirror. On the back, inside an inset of bluish-silver mother of pearl, were the initials:

V M .

"What a wonderful treasure," Christina said. "I wonder what the owner's name was?" *Christina knew she needed to find out, but she didn't know why it seemed so important.*

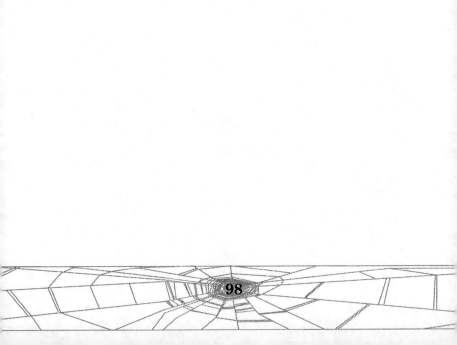

16
THE FIERCEST
PIRATE OF THEM ALL!

The sun shone straight overhead, heating up everything it fell upon, but the breeze coming over the ocean and around the front of the shipwrecked sailboat was cool. Christina, Grant, Sean, and Sally sat in the shade on the seashore side of the wreck.

"Sally, do you think you'll ever leave the Banks?" Christina asked.

"I don't think so," Sally said, "except maybe to go to college. I love it here, even if things are changing."

"How about you, Sean?" Christina asked.

"My dad is the fourth generation to man the lighthouse," Sean said.

"Are you going to be a lighthouse keeper too?" Christina asked.

"Naw!" Sean said. "They aren't needed that much anymore. I'm going to join the Coast Guard.

I want to save people like Sally's great, great granddaddy."

"Good," Grant said. "I'm glad you'll be around to rescue me if I need help when I'm treasure hunting!"

"Ha!" Sean said. "This is the perfect place for you to hunt treasure. Dad says there are plenty of wrecks still holding gold and other treasures, but they're buried deep under water and sand.

"In fact," Sean continued, "some people say that the famous pirate Blackbeard buried his treasure at the southern end of Ocracoke Island."

"Really?" Grant asked, his eyes lighting up. "Is that far from here? And why did he leave his treasure buried in the sand?"

"Ocracoke Island isn't far," Sally said. "And as for Blackbeard, he probably didn't get a chance to spend his treasure, because he died during an attack by government officials."

"Yeah!" Sean said, standing up, facing the three. "I'll tell you what happened to him! Blackbeard's ship, the *Adventure*, viciously attacked a British ship with cannon fire. But the *Adventure* ran aground. As the British ship pulled alongside it, Blackbeard's pirates tossed 'grenadoes,' or bottles filled with gunpowder, shot, and pieces of iron, onto the decks of the British ship. While the grenadoes exploded, Blackbeard and 15 of his pirates swarmed the ship."

Grant was riveted by the story. "What happened next?" he asked.

"They were met by the crew of the British ship," Sean said, "which had been hiding below deck, and a vicious fight broke out. Blackbeard got shot, but kept fighting. He was about to run his blade through the commander of the British ship, Lieutenant Maynard, when one of Maynard's men slashed his sword at the lunging pirate."

Sean whipped his stick downward, imitating the blow. "He cut a gash in his neck, but Blackbeard still fought on." Sean danced around the sand as if he was swordfighting.

"After being shot, stabbed, and wounded by swords, Blackbeard finally collapsed," Sean said, falling to the sand.

Suddenly, he sat straight up. "But just before going into battle, one of his men had asked him if his wife knew where his treasure was buried. Blackbeard said that only he and the devil knew where it was buried, and the longest liver should take it all!"

"The longest 'liver' should take it all?" Grant said. "What does that mean? It makes me think of that gross slimy thing in the Thanksgiving turkey!"

"You got me," Sean said. "You know I'm not good with riddles or knock, knock—did you hear that?"

SQUAWK! SQUAWK!

"It's that bird again," Grant said. "How did he get out here?"

"I think they're called wings," Christina said, as the bird landed on the edge of the boat above them.

"Hey, birdie," Sally said. "Does Polly want some seafood?"

"I don't think birds eat seafood," Grant said.

"Sure they do," Sally said. "Gulls, herons, and ospreys eat fish."

"I meant pretty colorful birds like this one," Grant said, watching the bird stare at them.

Look to the sea, for you're not alone.

Avast, ye maties!

The bird wagged his head back and forth, gazing at all of the kids. "Look to the sea, for you're not alone," it repeated.

"It's more of the riddle," Christina said.

"SquaWK!   SquaWK!"

squealed the bird as it took to the air.

"That's one talkative bird," Sean said.

"Hold on!" Sally said. "What was that about?"

"I think the bird is trying to tell us something," Christina said.

"Why us?" Grant asked. "Sean and Sally have lived here all their lives. Why doesn't the bird tell them? Why is the parrot giving us clues, anyway?"

"I don't know," Christina said. "Maybe it has tried to tell other people, but they didn't listen."

"Maybe it's concerned about something," Sean said, scratching his head.

Or someone, Christina thought.

"How does the riddle go again?" Sean asked, looking over at Christina.

Christina looked skyward. "The parts we have are, 'Survive the shoals, and you'll see it clearly. The beasts can't stop you, but they make you weary. Look to the sea, for you're not alone'."

"What does it mean?" Sally asked.

"I'm not totally sure—yet," Christina said. "But it seems like it should have at least one more line."

"Maybe," Grant suggested, "it's trying to lead us to Blackbeard's treasure!"

Christina's mind clicked into high gear once again. She knew what the beasts were, but how did it tie into the rest of the riddle? In the distance, she saw another rowboat. She looked closely—it was the hermit again! *Could he be a relative of Blackbeard? Was he trying to keep them from finding the treasure?*

17

THE EAGLE HAS LANDED

Mimi had big plans for the next day. First, she had set up a tour of the *Barque Eagle*. Then, she was taking everyone on a ferry ride around the Banks.

Grant followed Sean, Sally, Papa, Christina, and Mimi down the plank leading from the *Eagle* to the dock. They were all silent. As the only active, commissioned sailing vessel in any of the U.S. services, she was simply magnificent to behold.

The group stood in awe as a crew of young Coast Guard cadets hoisted all of the ship's 21,350 square feet of white sails. Sean was amazed at how fast the cadets yanked five miles of rigging to raise them.

The group stepped gingerly across the magnificent, three-inch-thick, teak wood that covered the forecastle, quarterdeck, and the weather decks. Sean watched the officers performing their duties. "I hope to be one of them in a few years," he said.

Mimi was the first to break the silence as the group toured the ship. "I didn't know this ship was originally a World War II Nazi training ship," she said, "and that after we defeated Germany in World War II, we took her as a war prize and renamed her the *Barque Eagle*."

"Oh," Christina said, "that's a better name than it had before, the *Horst Wessel*."

"Huh?" Grant asked. "Why would they name a pretty ship like this the *Horse Vessel*? Did they carry horses on it? If they did, they would have needed a really big pooper scooper!" he exclaimed, giggling at his own joke.

"No, Grant," Papa said, shaking his head at his silly grandson. "*Horst Wessel* was the name of a German song."

Grant shrugged. "Okay," he said. "But can you believe that kitchen? Those Coast Guard trainees have it made. There's so much food in those giant walk-in refrigerators and freezers. I wish Mom and Dad could buy one each of those. I'd never go hungry!"

"You never do go hungry!" Christina said.

"I don't think I've ever seen so many ropes in my life," Sally said.

"They're not called ropes," Sean s
group walked down the ramp and climb
the rental van. He turned around and looked ba
at the 295-foot ship. "It's called rigging."

"Whatever it's called, it was an incredible tour," Sally said. "Thank you, Mimi."

"You're both welcome," Mimi said. "Now, time for a ferry ride!"

Grant stiffened in his seat. "Fairy ride!" he exclaimed. "That's for babies! I'm not going on that!"

Mimi and Papa laughed. Papa tousled Grant's blond hair. "It's F-E-R-R-Y, Grant. That's a boat that takes you from place to place."

"Oh," Grant replied, settling back in the cool leather seat. "That's better. I'll do that."

"Make a left out of the lot, Mimi," Sean said. "And go four blocks and then make another left down to the dock."

"Are you sure you've done this before, Sean?" Mimi asked.

"Yes, ma'am," Sean said. "Sally and I ride the ferries all around the Banks. Our first stop is Shackleford Banks, then Ocracoke, and Hatteras. From there we take the bus up highway 12 back into town. There's a stop at the Lighthouse."

"Good," Mimi remarked. "Papa will need lots of places to rest. It's not easy walking around with a cast on your leg!"

Christina stared out the window. Maybe we'll find some answers on this trip, she thought. *What is that parrot trying to tell us?*

18

THOSE AREN'T REAL PONIES!

The ferry ride from Morehead City to Shackleford Banks was quick. Mimi and Papa decided to enjoy an ice cream cone while the kids went exploring.

"We have an hour before the ferry leaves for Ocracoke," Sean said. "You want to check out the wild ponies?"

"Wild ponies?" Grant said.

"Yeah," Sally said. "They've been here for hundreds of years. People say they swam to shore from sinking Spanish ships long before people landed around here. They're actually horses, not ponies, but they're only about four feet tall, so everyone calls them ponies."

"Now, that's my kind of horse," Grant said. "Are they far from here?"

"Nope!" Sean said, leading the kids down a road toward the ocean. "They're all over the island."

"Are they friendly?" Christina asked.

"Yes!" Sean said. "Unless you scare them."

Christina and Sally took off their shoes to stroll in the warm, grainy sand. The blue sky, cool breeze, and rippling surf was relaxing.

"This is so peaceful," Christina said. "No wonder the ponies like it here."

"That's why Sean and I like to come here a couple of times every summer," Sally said, watching the boys run and jump in the sand. "They're such goofs."

Christina noticed that Sean and Grant had stopped their running and were crouched down by the marsh. "What are they up to?" she said.

Sean turned around and motioned for them to hurry over. "You've got to see this!" he shouted.

"Oh, my," Sally said, as she pulled up next to Grant. "Sea turtle eggs! Baby turtles are so cute!"

"Yep," Sean said, "and it looks like they're getting ready to hatch and head out to sea. Their mother laid the nest about two months ago."

"How do you know that?" Grant asked.

"Loggerhead turtles lay their nests in May and June and it takes about 60 to 70 days for them to hatch," Sean said, knocking Grant's hand away as he was reaching to grab one of the eggs. "Don't touch them; they need to make their way to the ocean once they hatch."

"I wanted to take one home with us," Grant said.

"It's illegal to take them," Sean said. "They're on the endangered species list, so no one is supposed to disturb them."

"These poor little things," Christina said, looking at the cute eggs. "They have to go out into that big, scary ocean all by themselves?"

"Yep!" Sally said. "And only one in 1,000 will survive to maturity."

Christina saw a small sailboat in the distance. I wonder what the hermit's up to, she thought. The last clue popped into her head. "Look to the sea, for you're not alone." She scanned the beach. "Are we alone?" she wondered.

She didn't see the pair of eyes watching all of them through thick, black binoculars.

19
WHAT A RIDE!

FFFPPPPPTTTTT!

Sean heard a noise behind him and turned. A pair of curious brown eyes stared at him. Strands of scraggly hair hung over one eye. Then, the horse looked down and stomped its right hoof into the sand, digging a hole.

Grant walked up to Sean. "What's it doing?" Grant asked.

"It's digging a water hole so it can drink," Sally said.

"Wouldn't the water be salty?" Grant asked.

"No," Sean said. "The salt gets filtered out by the soil beneath the sand. It would be a little salty for us, but the horses don't mind it."

Grant heard another horse neighing. He ran over a hill toward the sound. When he reached the top, he stood on a ledge overlooking a flat sandy area where six horses stood. One of them was just below him.

"Grant," Sean said, "don't move."

Grant spun around. "Don't what—" he said. His eyes fell on a coiled six-foot brown and tan snake. Its triangular head told him it was poisonous.

"Oh!" Grant sensed the snake was going to strike and took a step backwards.

"WHOOAAAA!"

As the snake uncoiled, Grant fell backwards. He landed right on the back of a spotted pony. The startled horse neighed and raced down the beach with Grant clinging to its matted mane. Sean, Christina, and Sally tried to catch up, but couldn't as Grant disappeared over a dune.

RING! RING!

It was Mimi calling. She and Papa were still resting at the visitor's center. "What am I going to tell Mimi?" Christina said to Sean.

"Tell her we're racing to catch Grant and you'll call her right back!" Sean cried.

Grant clutched the horse's neck as it galloped one way, then reversed direction, and frantically raced in another. It bucked and jumped into the air, launching Grant face first into a fluffy sand dune.

"Grant!" Christina yelled. Her brother rolled over to see Christina, Sean, and Sally staring down at him. They burst out laughing.

"What's so funny?" Grant asked. "I just got thrown from a horse! Or pony! Or whatever it is!"

"You look like the 'Sandman'," Sean said, giggling. "You are so sweaty, you have sand stuck all over you! It looks like you have a mask on your face!"

PFFFTTT!

Grant sat up and spit sand out of his mouth. "I *was* hungry," he said, "but not for a sand sandwich!"

The ferry whistle blew and the children rushed down the beach to get back on the ferry.

Mimi noticed piles of sand pouring out of Grant's shorts onto his seat. "It looks like you had a good time on the beach!" she said.

Grant just smiled, still grinding grains of sand between his teeth. "I did, Mimi!" he replied. "I really did!"

20
THE BEASTS

Christina, Grant, Sean, and Sally leaned on the rail at the back of the ferry. Mimi and Papa decided to take a bus back to the beach house. Papa's leg was bothering him. The ferry operator had promised to keep an eye on the kids.

"There's not many people on the ferry this afternoon," Sally said.

"It's early," Sean said. "There will be more on the next one."

SQUAWK!   SQUAWK!

"I don't believe it," Grant said. "That bird found us this far from Hatteras?"

The parrot landed on a railing near Christina and Grant. Its feathers were coated in salty sea spray.

The bird's feathers fluttered in a gust of wind. "Cling to your memories, for they're all you own," it repeated. As it leaped into the air, flapping its wings, it coasted past the front of the ferry and disappeared.

"That's Hatteras Inlet way up there," Sean explained, pointing in the direction the parrot had flown. "We should be at Hatteras in about half an hour. Did you get what the parrot said?"

"Yes," Christina replied, "It said, 'Cling to your memories, for they're all you own'."

"It still doesn't make any sense," Grant said.

"Guys," Sally said, looking behind the ferry, "the sky is getting really dark behind us. It looks like it's going to rain."

"It does," Grant said, "and the fog is beginning to roll in too."

Sean scanned the darkened sky. "That storm came up fast," he said. "We had better take cover."

Moments later, fat raindrops began to pelt the ferry's deck.

As the storm worsened quickly, the steward thrust life vests into everyone's hands. Sean and Sally helped Christina and Grant fasten their vests just before a powerful wind gust pushed them into each other. Grant wrapped his arms around Christina and held onto a pole supporting the ferry's canvas top. Sean did the same thing with Sally.

They were about to pass by the Hatteras Inlet when the ferry turned into Pamlico Sound. Sean winced when he saw a growing wave barreling through the inlet. It broke up before crossing their path, but the ferry rocked violently. A man fell and slid off the deck into the water!

"Man overboard!" someone shouted.

Grant tightened his grip on the pole. The ferry continued to rock and roll on the waves.

"Oh, no!" cried Sean. "Another wave! Hold on!"

A mountain of frothy water crashed into the ferry, tilting it on its side. Grant and Christina held on with every ounce of strength they had. As the ferry topped the wave, they fell back toward the pole.

Grant heard Sean shouting and pointing at another wave on its way. Grant just stared at it, wide-eyed.

"Head to the bow and jump over the rail!" the steward shouted to the passengers. "The ferry might flip over!"

Sean, Sally, Grant, and Christina scrambled to the bow railing, sliding on the slippery deck. Sean and Sally leaped into the water without looking back.

Grant grabbed Christina's hand. "Let's do this!" he shouted. They flung themselves into the water and swam after Sean and Sally.

CRUNCH!

CRASH!

SPLASH!

They all turned in time to see the wave hit the starboard side of the ferry. This time it flipped over.

"Grab on! Grab on!" a deep voice shouted. Christina spied the rowboat in front of them and pushed Grant toward it. She saw someone in a bright yellow hooded raincoat drag him into the boat. The same yellow arm then yanked her into the boat in one swift move, right past the faded name on the boat's bow, *Making Music*.

The hooded figure then pulled Sean and Sally into the boat. Other boats joined in the rescue, and soon all the passengers and crew were plucked from the water.

The man in the hooded raincoat never spoke as he helped the children back to shore. Christina looked back to thank him, but he was already rowing away.

A movement in the air caught her eye. Was that the parrot flying over the rowboat?

21
OUTER BANKS ANGEL

Mimi stepped onto the deck of the rental house, holding a steaming hot mug of coffee. Papa followed close behind on his crutches, letting the screen door slam shut behind him.

It was another beautiful morning. The sky was deep blue and small waves rolled lazily onto the beach, a stark difference from yesterday's storm.

"What are you doing?" Mimi asked. Christina sat cross-legged in a deck chair. She was writing on one of Mimi's writing pads. Grant peered over her shoulder from his perch on the railing.

"We're figuring out the clues to the riddle the Macaw began to give us the night we landed," Christina said.

"Began?" Papa said. "What do you mean, began?"

"Since that first night, the Macaw has given us three more clues," Christina said.

"When?" Mimi asked, taking a sip of her coffee.

"Once when we were combing the beach for shells with Sean," Grant explained, "then we got another when we were at the shipwreck, and the last one came when we were on the ferry yesterday."

"So," Papa said, "what have you gleaned from the clues?"

"It's about the Outer Banks Angel," Christina said.

"Really?" Mimi asked.

Christina repeated the entire riddle:

"Survive the shoals, and you'll see it clearly,
The beasts can't stop you, but they make you weary.
Look to the sea, for you're not alone,
Cling to your memories, for they're all you own."

"Okay," Papa said. "What do you think it means?"

"It means," Christina explained, "that he survived a shipwreck, and he knows that his purpose in life is to save people from other shipwrecks. But although the storms, or the beasts, can't stop him, over time he's growing tired of fighting them."

"He was a storm survivor," Grant said. "But now he rescues others from the sea, and because he's there to help, those people are not alone. And no matter how bleak things are, there's always hope. You keep hope alive by clinging to your memories, because they're all you truly own."

"Wow!" Papa exclaimed. "I think you two will do well in your high school English classes when you have to **decipher** the meanings of poems."

"That's true," Mimi said. "But the riddle doesn't tell you who it is or that it's the Outer Banks Angel. Besides, he's been around for a long time."

"Exactly," Christina said. "That's where we had to use other smaller clues we gathered during the last five days. We think the riddle is about the old hermit who lives up the beach near the lighthouse. He's the OBA!"

"Why do you think that?" Mimi asked.

"Do you remember Lieutenant Bailey saying that for the first few years, the Angel's voice was that of a girl?" Christina asked.

"Yes," Mimi answered, peering over her sparkly red reading glasses.

"It wasn't a girl's voice at all," Christina maintained. "It was a boy's voice, like Grant's, before it changed when he became a teenager."

"Hey," Grant remarked, in the deepest voice he could. "I've got a deep voice." He flexed his scrawny bicep muscles. "And big man muscles," he added.

"I see," Papa said. "That means he's now an old man."

"Yes," Christina said. "Sean said the hermit's been living on the Banks since before Sean's dad was born. Yesterday, when the man pulled us from the water, he never showed us his face. He never even looked back."

Christina stood up, waving her pencil. "He didn't want us to know who he was," she added. "The faded name on the boat was *Making Music*. Sean said that his dad called the hermit MM."

"Okay," Mimi said. "So you think MM stands for *Making Music* and not his name?"

"Right," Christina said. "We researched shipwrecks off the Banks over the last 80 years. About 60 years ago, a wealthy family went missing when their sailing yacht sank in a storm near Diamond Shoals.

"The only person the Coast Guard couldn't account for was the family's eight-year-old son," Christina continued. "They never found him or the yacht's rowboat. We found a picture of the yacht online, because it had won several sailing races.

The name on the stern was *Making Music*. The family's name was Mason. They lived in Virginia. The boy's name was Thomas."

Christina folded her arms across her chest. "I'm sure the hermit is Thomas!" she declared.

130

22
MASON'S BOY

"Wow," Papa said. "I am really proud of you two. It sounds like you have figured out the parrot's riddle!"

"Yes!" Mimi said, "but we need to tell the Coast Guard what you've figured out."

"Why?" Grant asked. "If Thomas wanted people to know who he was, he would have told them."

"I agree, Grant," Christina said, "but there's got to be a reason why the parrot wanted us to know."

"The parrot?" Grant said. "How can the parrot know anything? He's just a bird."

"A remarkable old bird," Papa said. "Parrots live a very long time. And many pets sense that their owners are sick or something is wrong with them. I think we need to talk with this hermit."

"There's only one problem," Mimi said. "He may be an old man now, but if he shipwrecked when he was eight, he may only have the mind of a child."

"Oh my gosh!" Christina said. "I hadn't thought of that. That would explain his behavior. He acts like he doesn't like children, but then we've seen him following us everywhere. He wanted to protect us."

"He's probably been through a lot of rough things in his life," Mimi said. "Maybe all of it is making him weary."

"Papa," said Christina, "You're right. We do need to talk to him, but I think it should just be Grant and me, so we don't scare him."

"That's okay with me," Papa said, "but we'll be close by. I've got an idea too."

23
THANK YOU

Christina and Grant slowly approached Thomas' shelter. He was sitting with his back to them, talking to the Macaw.

"Here, birdie," Thomas said, holding out food scraps for the Macaw. "Eat up. That's all I've got today."

Thomas pulled out an old, tattered piece of paper. "Do you want me to read my poem again?" he asked. "I know you've heard it many times over the years."

The Macaw tilted his head and blinked his eyes.

> "Survive the shoals, and you'll see it clearly,
> The beasts can't stop you, but they make you weary.
> Look to the sea, for you're not alone,
> Cling to your memories, for they're all you own."

Christina and Grant looked at each other. It wasn't a riddle. It was a poem! After Thomas repeated the poem several times, Christina stepped forward.

"Mister M," Christina said.

Thomas jumped. "WHAT ARE YOU DOING HERE?" he screamed.

"This is my beach! You get out of here, right now!" he said. "I don't like guests, and I especially don't like children. SHOO! SHOO!"

"It's okay, Thomas, Thomas Mason," Christina said.

The man stared at Christina in amazement. He slowly raised his head. "How do you know me? I haven't heard my name in a long time."

"We know what happened to you a long time ago," Grant said.

"We wanted to thank you for rescuing us," Christina said. "And for rescuing all those other people through the years. You've made a difference in many lives, and I know your parents would be proud of you."

Thomas looked stunned.

Christina reached into her pocket and pulled out the mirror she had found in the shipwreck. "I just have a feeling," she said, "that this might belong to you." She gently handed the mirror to Thomas.

Thomas fingered the mirror with his bony, tanned fingers. A single tear appeared in his eye. It slowly spilled over and ran down his cheek.

"That's my mother's mirror," he whispered. "Her name was Victoria, Victoria Mason." He tried to rub away the flood of tears that began to flow down both cheeks.

"We're here to help you," Grant said. "And a lot of other people want to help you too, because you've helped them."

Papa and Mimi stepped out from behind a sand dune.

Thomas began to back up. "It's okay," Christina said, gently grabbing his hand and pulling him forward. "This is our grandma and grandpa."

Papa reached out his hand to Thomas. "Thank you, Thomas," Papa said, shaking Thomas's hand.

A young couple stepped forward. "You might not remember us," the man said, "but you saved us from our sinking boat, just six months ago."

"Thank you," the woman said. "If it wasn't for you, we wouldn't be here today."

Suddenly, a line of people appeared, stretching out around the dune. They each came forward to thank the Outer Banks Angel for rescuing them. Lieutenant Bailey stood away from the group, watching the emotional scene. He had the biggest grin on his face that Grant and Christina had ever seen.

SQUAWK! SQUAWK!

Christina looked up to see the Macaw parrot hovering over her and Grant. It slowly set itself down on Grant's shoulder. Christina looked shocked, then smiled at the bird. "We got your message, old buddy," she said. "We got it!"

"I can't wait to tell Sean and Sally!" Grant said, keeping his voice low so he didn't spook the parrot. "They just won't believe it!"

24
HOME, SWEET HOME

The flight back to Peachtree City, Georgia was smooth, proving that the *Mystery Girl* was back in good condition. Papa taxied the plane to a stop at Falcon Field, and announced, "Home, sweet home!"

"I'm really going to miss Sean and Sally," Grant said.

"Me too," Christina added.

"I have an idea," Mimi said. "I'll talk to their parents and see if they can come and visit over the Thanksgiving break. After what you two did, you deserve a reward."

"Mimi," Christina said, "do you think Thomas is going to be okay?"

"I talked to Lieutenant Bailey before we left, and he said Thomas is doing just fine," Mimi answered. "He has some health problems, so Lieutenant Bailey found a place for him to live and a way for him to earn some money helping out on the Coast Guard base."

"I still can't believe that the riddle was a poem Thomas wrote about his life," Grant said. "The parrot was just repeating it to us, and it turned out to be just what we needed to figure out who the Outer Banks Angel was!"

"You're right!" Christina said. "I'm so glad we helped him. He has helped *so many* other people."

"You kids figured out something very important," Papa said. "In more than 60 years, no one else had figured out who the Outer Banks Angel was, except you two. I am quite impressed!"

Grant and Christina gave each other a high-five. "Just another day in the life of mystery solvers!" Grant exclaimed. He rubbed his tummy. "So, what's for lunch?"

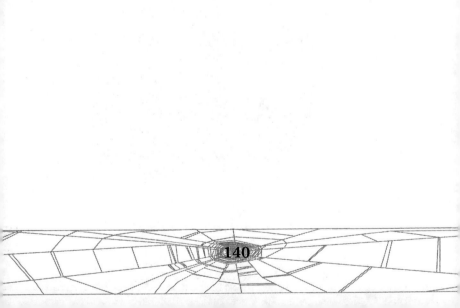

Now...go to

www.carolemarshmysteries.com
and...

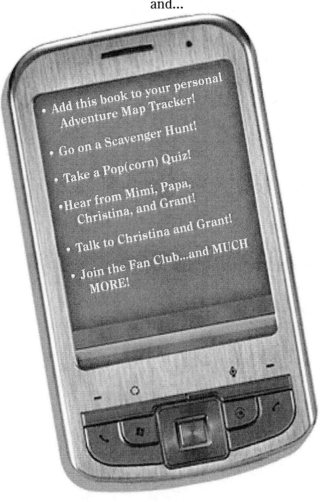

- Add this book to your personal Adventure Map Tracker!

- Go on a Scavenger Hunt!

- Take a Pop(corn) Quiz!

- Hear from Mimi, Papa, Christina, and Grant!

- Talk to Christina and Grant!

- Join the Fan Club...and MUCH MORE!

GLOSSARY

anonymous: something that has no known name or identity

cowl: a sheet metal cover fitted around an engine

helm: steering device for a ship

plunder: to rob; take illegally

saunter: walk leisurely; stroll

shoal: an area of the sea that is shallow

SAT GLOSSARY

acclimate: get used to a certain climate

decipher: to convert some type of code, or to figure out difficult handwriting

navigation: the science of figuring the path of a ship or an airplane

penetrate: to pass into or through; pierce

prejudice: dislike or distrust of people just because they are of another race, religion, or nationality

GRAVEYARD OF THE ATLANTIC TRIVIA

1. Richard Etheridge, the first black keeper in the U.S. Lifesaving Service, was born to a slave named Rachel Dough. She lived in the household of John Etheridge. John taught Richard to read and write even though it was illegal to do so.

2. Richard Etheridge's gravesite is on the grounds of the North Carolina Aquarium on Roanoke Island.

3. More than 600 ships have sunk off the North Carolina Outer Banks.

4. Consisting of shifting sand bars, Diamond Shoals extends 14 miles out into the Atlantic Ocean.

5. Residents of the Outer Banks are known as "Outer Bankers."

6. During World War II, German U-boats sank many Allied tankers and cargo ships along the Outer Banks. The area became known as Torpedo Junction.

7. Few ships wreck on the Outer Banks today, but the ruins of old shipwrecks are still exposed by storms from time to time.

8. The Cape Hatteras lighthouse is the tallest lighthouse in the nation!

Enjoy this exciting excerpt from:

THE MYSTERY OF THE HAUNTED GHOSTTOWN
1 BITING THE DUST

"Ghost towns! Are we going to see real ghost towns?" Grant asked his grandfather, Papa. "And REAL ghosts in the ghost towns?"

"Could be," replied Papa, as he checked the gages of his little red and white airplane, the *Mystery Girl,* preparing the plane for landing.

"Grant, there ARE no ghosts in ghost towns!" his sister, Christina, claimed in an older-sister, bossy way, as she tugged one of his blond curls. "I told you that! Papa, you're just leading Grant on!"

"Don't be too sure about that, Christina," Papa answered, with a twinkle in his eye. "I've been in ghost towns, and I'd swear I came across a ghost or two! Those towns just might be haunted." He laughed and added, "You'll see for yourself!"

"You'll have to make a believer out of me!" Christina declared, her arms thrust across her chest. She thought visiting ghost towns would be exciting, but certainly not scary. Sitting silently, her finger twirling a lock of her brown hair and her tongue toying with the braces on her teeth, Christina wondered if Papa was right. She suspected he would tease her in some ghost town, probably acting like a ghost to scare her, just to prove his point. I'll have to keep an eye on him, Christina thought.

Christina and Grant often traveled with their grandparents. Their grandmother, Mimi, wrote mysteries for children, and often needed to do research in fascinating locations around the world. This trip, however, was a vacation. "There are no mysteries on my agenda, thank you very much!" Mimi had said when she invited the kids to come along.

Papa knew a lot about the Old West, and was something of a cowboy, always wearing jeans, a cowboy hat, and cowboy boots. With his stories of the Old West, Papa had no trouble convincing the kids to take this vacation in southern Arizona. They had looked forward to this trip for a long time, and now the day had finally come!

Mimi was not as thrilled. There was all that heat! And sun! And dust! She loved wearing hats and sparkly red sunglasses, and now had a good reason to wear them both—to protect her blond hair and fair skin from the blazing sun!

What Mimi did love was the scenery of the West. The stark desert, with its prickly cacti and multi-colored sunsets, stole her heart every time she saw it. Plus, she couldn't wait to get her hands on the stunning pieces of jewelry handcrafted by the Native Americans!

The *Mystery Girl* slowly descended to land at a local airport near Tombstone, Arizona. The plane was now low enough so the kids could see details on the ground below.

Christina gazed out the window on her side of the plane. Immediately below, there was nothing but dry and dusty yellow land, covered in spots by some low, drab shrub brush. Here and there, tumbleweeds lazily drifted in the sandy soil.

Grant's blue eyes popped open wide. "Is that Boot Hill Cemetery over there?" he yelled, jabbing his finger against the window on his side of the plane.

"Sure is," Papa said. "That's the real thing!"

"Wow—that's where the gunslingers are buried! Can we go there, Papa?" Grant asked, jumping up and down in his seat despite being **constrained** by his seat belt.

"It's just a bunch of tombstones," Christina remarked. She thought her little brother was silly to get so excited over an old cemetery. "You can see tombstones anywhere."

"Not like these," Papa said, with another of those twinkles in his eye. "You'll see!"

"OK, Papa...I suppose ghosts pop out from behind the tombstones and talk to you," Christina said. "Can't wait to see that!" She glanced out the window again to see a cloud of dust envelop the plane. Pebbles from the dirt runway rocketed everywhere, pelting the plane as it touched down.

Against the backdrop of the coffee-colored soil, Christina spotted a dark brown steer struggling to stand. Each time it got up, the bull collapsed again in a cloud of dust. The animal's legs were too weak for it to stand. A flock of buzzards slowly circled overhead.

Christina couldn't imagine a more **desolate** scene. She felt goose bumps on her neck. Maybe it wasn't just the ghost towns that were haunted, she thought. Maybe the whole place was haunted!

Little did she know how scary things could get in a ghost town—and a cemetery! This steer in distress was just the beginning of an Old West mystery!

Enjoy this exciting excerpt from:

THE GHOST OF THE GOLDEN GATE BRIDGE
1 A FOGGY LANDING

"Papa, I thought you said we were 'bringing this plane down' a few minutes ago and that we were almost to San Francisco. So why are there still clouds?" Christina asked her grandfather.

"I am bringing us down, Christina," Papa replied, as he guided his small red and white airplane into San Francisco airspace. "We're not in clouds, we're in fog. Didn't you know that San Francisco is famous for the fog that comes in from the ocean during the summer?"

"But you can't see a thing, Papa!" exclaimed Christina, brushing her long brown hair over her shoulder and rubbing her tongue over the new braces on her teeth.

"Maybe Papa has X-ray vision," said Grant, Christina's blond, curly-haired little brother. He pulled his blue eyes wide open with his fingers and stared at Christina.

"Stop that, Grant!" Christina ordered. "You're not helping things!"

Mimi, Christina and Grant's grandmother, sensed Christina's anxiety. "Don't worry, Christina," she said calmly. "You know that Papa is the best pilot in the whole world and the *Mystery Girl* always takes us safely wherever we want to go."

"Oh, I know," Christina said, nodding her head. "This fog just gives me a creepy feeling."

Christina and Grant often joined their grandparents on trips—all over the United States—and to other countries, too! Mimi, a children's mystery book writer, often traveled to her book locations to do research.

But this time, Mimi wanted to relax and visit with some friends, Mr. and Mrs. Chambers, in San Francisco. Plus, she knew the children would love San Francisco, one of the most exotic and exciting cities in the world! The children enjoyed traveling with Mimi and Papa, and somehow their trips always became an adventure!

The wispy fog outside Christina's window seemed to grow thicker with each passing minute.

"When are we going to land?" she asked, her hands clenched.

Papa decided to divert Christina's attention. "Christina, listen. I have a song for you," he said.

"You do?" she asked in anticipation.

"Yep, here goes!" Papa began singing in his loudest baritone voice, "I left my heart . . . in San Francisco . . . high on a hill . . . it calls to me . . . "

Mimi beamed. "I always did like that song!" she exclaimed, patting Papa on the shoulder.

Grant interrupted Papa's serenade. "Look! I see something . . . there . . . in the fog . . . it's something red!" he exclaimed. "Is that the bridge you told us to look for?"

"Yes, that's it!" exclaimed Mimi.

"Oh, it's beautiful!" Christina said. "But the way it's mostly hidden in the fog . . . there's something sort of . . . well, mysterious about it."

"Oh, sweetie," Mimi said with a sigh, "remember, I'm here strictly for pleasure—I don't want to even hear the word 'mysterious' used around me this week! Okay?"

"It's awesome!" shouted Grant. "But . . . it's not gold," he added, disappointed. "I thought you said it was a *golden* bridge!"

"It's named the Golden Gate Bridge, but it's not made of gold or even painted gold," explained Mimi. "Many years ago, a man named the opening where the mouth of the San Francisco Bay meets the Pacific Ocean the 'Golden Gate.' So, when the bridge was built to cross this opening, they decided to call it the Golden Gate Bridge."

"We're here!" Christina announced, as the *Mystery Girl's* tires softly touched the runway. Papa looked at Christina and winked. "I'm glad to get out of that soup, too!" he remarked.

Papa plopped his cowboy hat on his head and reached for Mimi's hand. "Let's get out and stretch our legs, shall we?"

2

THE BRIDGE THAT COULDN'T BE BULIT

"Welcome to San Francisco!" A young boy and girl shouted the greeting as they bounded across the runway toward the *Mystery Girl*. The children were Asian, with coffee-colored skin and dark, sparkling brown eyes. The girl's long, black hair glistened in the sun. An older man and woman hurried behind them.

"What a pleasant surprise for you to meet us here!" exclaimed Mimi, as a gust of wind tipped her wide-brimmed red hat, revealing the short blond curls underneath. She turned to Christina and Grant. "This is Mr. and Mrs. Chambers and their two grandchildren!" She buried Mrs. Chambers in a bear hug while Papa and Mr.

Chambers shook hands and slapped each other on the back.

"Look at you!" declared Mr. Chambers as he scrutinized Papa. "Still wearing jeans, cowboy boots, and a cowboy hat, I see! But are you still the free-spirited **maverick** I once knew?" Mr. Chambers asked Papa.

"You bet!" Papa replied. "Still as untamed and free . . . just galloping a little slower is all!"

"We couldn't wait to see you!" Mrs. Chambers panted as she tried to catch her breath. "We decided to have our chauffeur, Mr. Wong, drive us all here. Plus, our grandchildren, Scott and Lynn, were anxious to meet Christina and Grant. Scott and Lynn will be staying with us this week. Oh, I've got lots of plans to keep these kids entertained!"